MW00563758

LIBRA

PRESS

AN ABC OF CHILDHOOD TRAGEDY

———————

ISBN: 9781955858090

PUBLISHED BY LIBRA PRESS
507 CALLES ST SUITE #107, AUSTIN, TX 78702
LIBRARY *of* CONGRESS CONTROL
NUMBER: 2022930110

ILLUSTRATED AND DESIGNED BY JULIETTE FOGRA
ALL IMAGES COURTESY OF JULIETTE FOGRA

An ABC of Childhood Tragedy

VOLUME I

⌃⌃⌃

Dr. Jordan B Peterson

ILLUSTRATED / DESIGNED BY JULIETTE FOGRÂ

AS YOU'VE NEVER SEEN IT

CHILDHOOD

PETERSON & FOGRA CO-PRODUCTION

VOL. I

TO MY FATHER,
WALTER MILTON PETERSON,
WHO TAUGHT ME TO READ
AND TO LOVE BOOKS.

TABLE of CONTENTS

A

B

C

D

E

F

G

H

I

J

K

L

M

N

O

P

Q

R

S

T

U

V

W

X

Y

Z

About
the author

About
the illustrator

A

Adella, an abusive sprat
was fond of teasing little brats
they finally jumped her one fine day
and now Adella's locked away.

ADELLA. AN ABUSIVE SPRAT

B

Bertram was a bestial thug
he had a very brutal mug
he made a break for boarding school
where he thrived on being cruel

BERTRAM WAS A BESTIAL THUG

B

C

Cynthia constantly crabbed and cried
and then one day just up and died
her family all sympathized
but felt relieved so deep inside

CYNTHIA CONSTANTLY CRABBED AND CRIED

D

Dick was a damaged little boy
whose prancing father made him coy
when he ended up in jail
all competed for his tail

DICK WAS A DAMAGED LITTLE BOY

E

Elijah's step-mom, quite the sot
made of him a bitter tot
with no children of her own
teased him till he bled and groaned

ELIJAH'S STEP-MOM. QUITE THE SOT

F

Frederick was sadly flawed
after he was madly pawed
by his neighbour, deeply odd
where the hell was Christian God?

J. Fogrā

FREDERICK WAS SADLY FLAWED

F

G

Granville's grasping grandmother
gave her constant grief
she criticized poor Granville greatly
and afforded no relief

GRANVILLE'S GRASPING GRANDMOTHER

H

Hester's hapless happenstance
made her homicidal
it was either harm her mother
or wax most suicidal

HESTER'S HAPLESS HAPPENSTANCE

H

I

Isaiah embodied idiocy
but he hoped that he'd get free
from the priest's kind buggery
though his corpse could hardly flee

I

ISAIAH EMBODIED IDIOCY

I

J

Jessamine, a joyless dolt
was given forty thousand volts
by her jealous little sister
but when she died nobody missed her

JESSAMINE A JOYLESS DOLT

J

K

Katie's hair was kind of kurly
and her teeth were kind of pearly
but her skin was kind of knurly
and she remained an ugly girlie

KATIE'S HAIR WAS KIND OF KURLY

L

Leander was lumpish and listless and lacking
she learned to smoke when she was nine
at twelve years old her chronic hacking
doomed her to a box of pine

LEANDER WAS LUMPISH AND LISTLESS AND LACKING

M

Mildred Masheck's mother cracked
and fell upon her daughter's back
with malevolent intent
she rendered her short life misspent

MIDLRED MASHECK'S MOTHER CRACKED

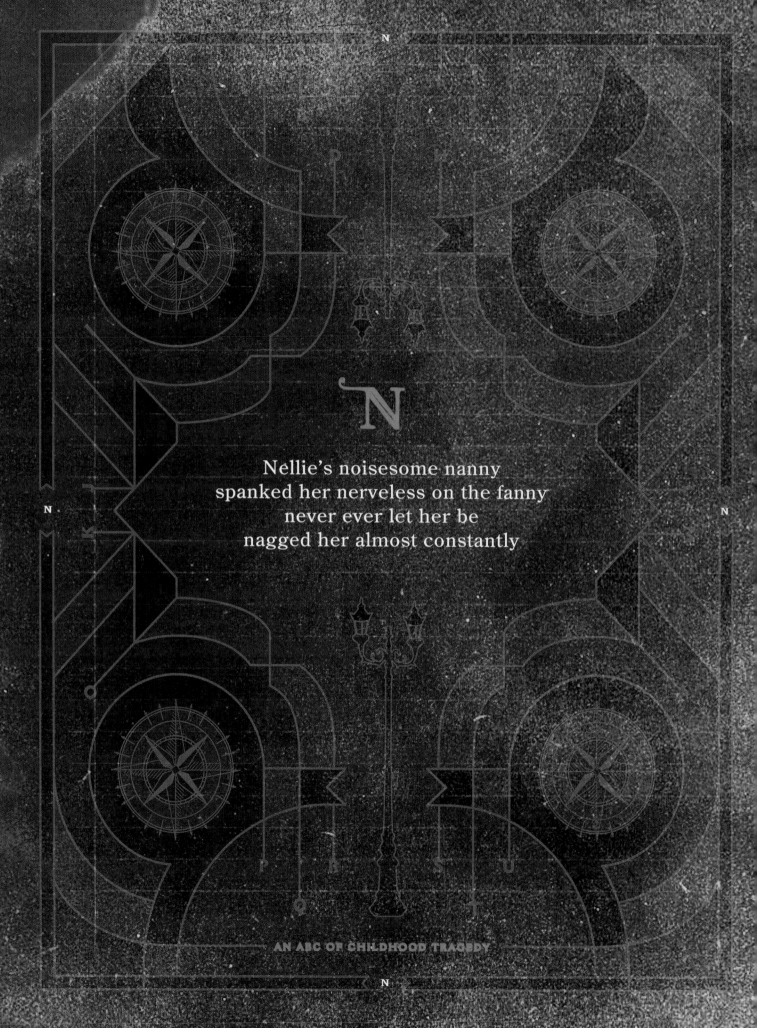

N

Nellie's noisesome nanny
spanked her nerveless on the fanny
never ever let her be
nagged her almost constantly

NELLIE'S NOISESOME NANNY

O

Oscar's oafish father's views
and his onslaughts of harsh abuse
his words that couldn't but confuse
left poor Oscar quite obtuse

OSCAR'S OAFISH FATHER'S VIEWS

O

P

Polly had a pretty dolly
that she pushed inside a trolley
a strange intruder pinched her doll
and used it to ensure her fall

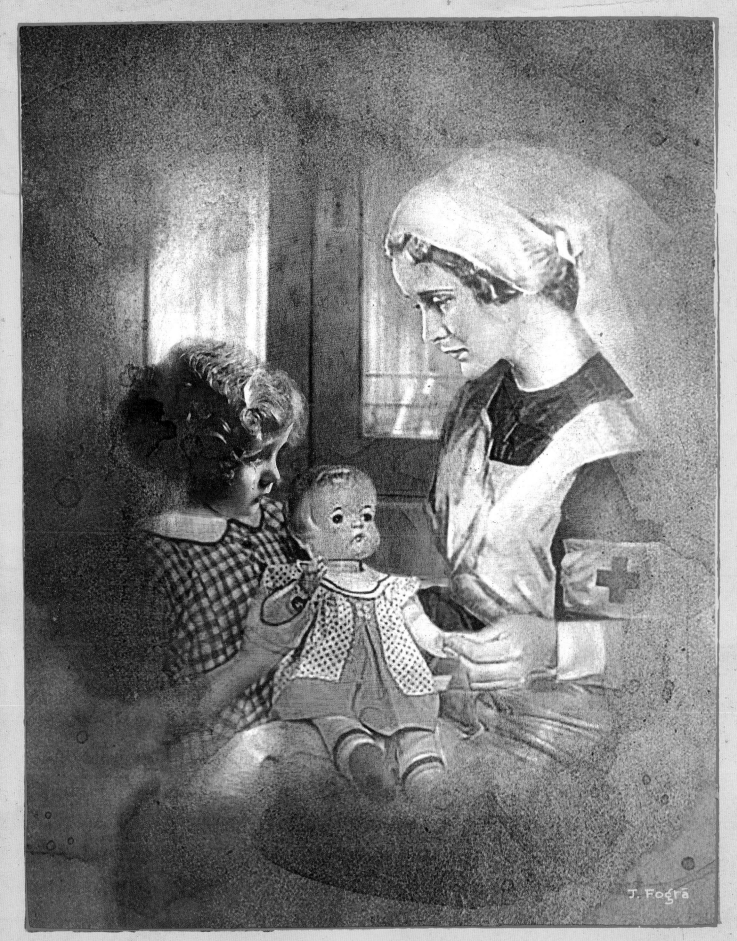

POLLY HAD A PRETTY DOLLY

Q

Quincy's querulous quibbling
and his constant shivering
forced his uncle's delivering
the blow that quelled his quivering

QUINCY'S QUERULOUS QUIBBLING

R

Reuben was a feckless rat
who rapped his mother with a bat
and then he stabbed her in the eye
no one who knew her wondered why

REUBEN WAS A FECKLESS RAT

S

Samuel squabbled sneerfully
and then complained most tearfully
when the children cheerfully
bullied him so jeerfully

AN ABC OF CHILDHOOD TRAGEDY

SAMUEL SQUABBLED SNEERFULLY

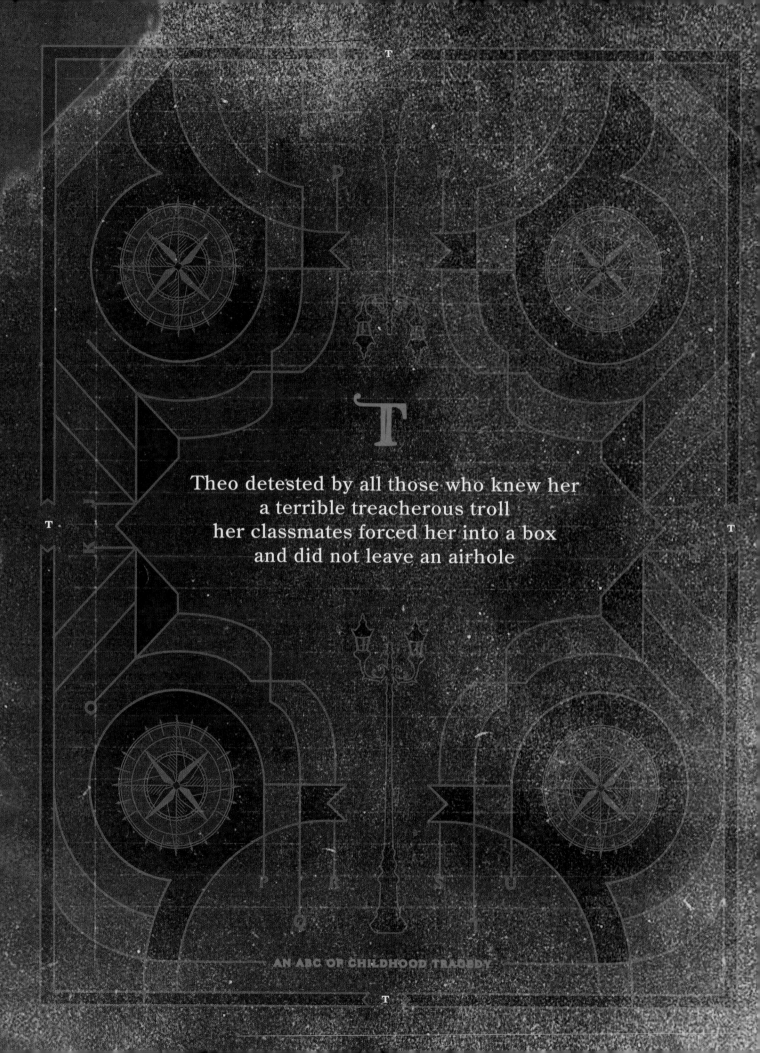

T

Theo detested by all those who knew her
a terrible treacherous troll
her classmates forced her into a box
and did not leave an airhole

THEO DETESTED BY ALL THOSE WHO KNEW HER

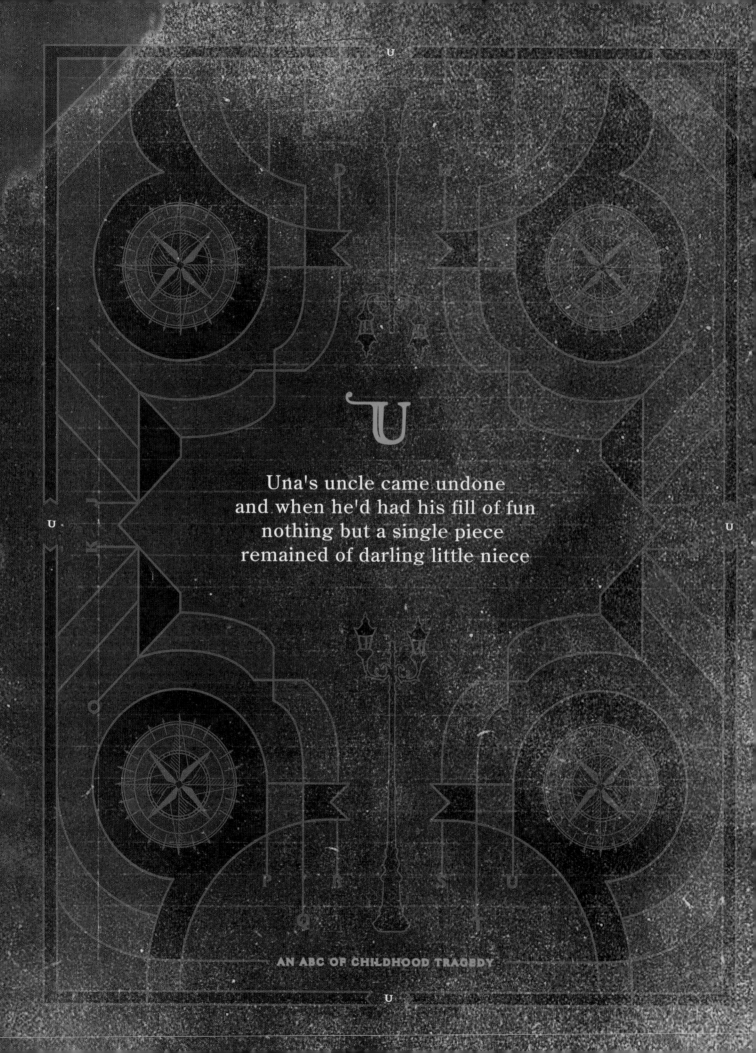

U

Una's uncle came undone
and when he'd had his fill of fun
nothing but a single piece
remained of darling little niece

AN ABC OF CHILDHOOD TRAGEDY

UNA'S UNCLE CAME UNDONE

U

V

When Vertiline was just a child
her mother, vulgar, vain and vile
left her for someone worthwhile
let her grow up void and wild

WHEN VERTILINE WAS JUST A CHILD

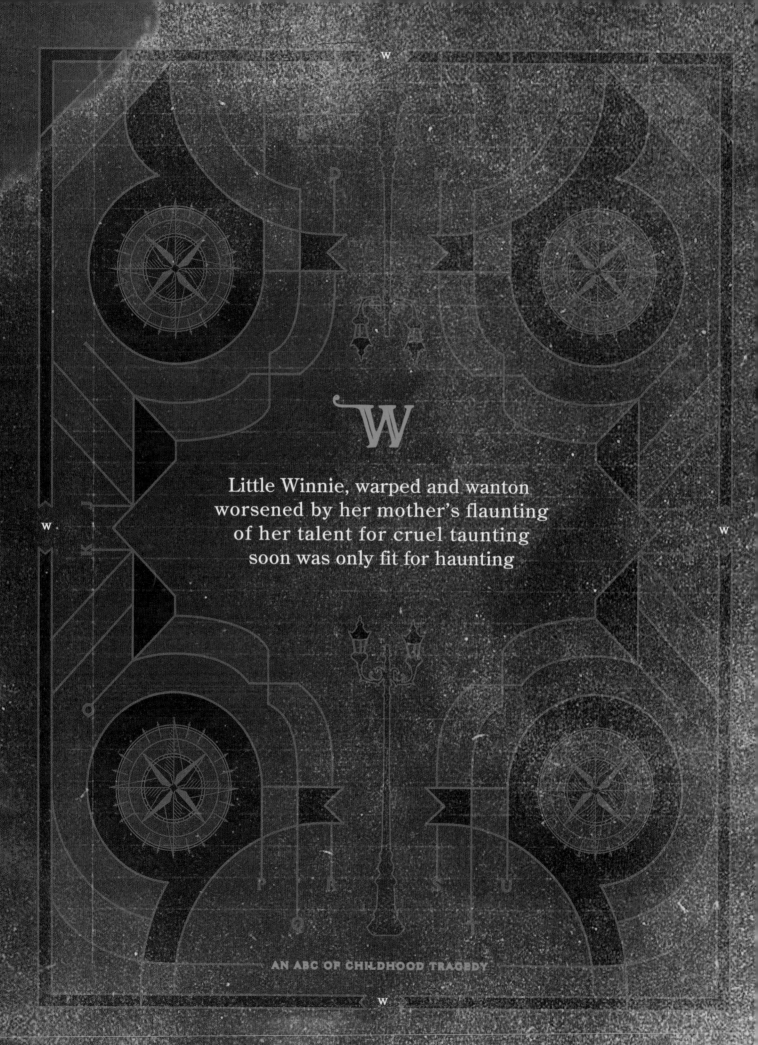

Little Winnie, warped and wanton
worsened by her mother's flaunting
of her talent for cruel taunting
soon was only fit for haunting

AN ABC OF CHILDHOOD TRAGEDY

LITTLE WINNIE. WARPED AND WANTON

W

X

Xandra xisted on a shoestring
and xcelled at blithering
her old father had enough
and what he did was rather rough

XANDRA XISTED ON A SHOESTRING

X

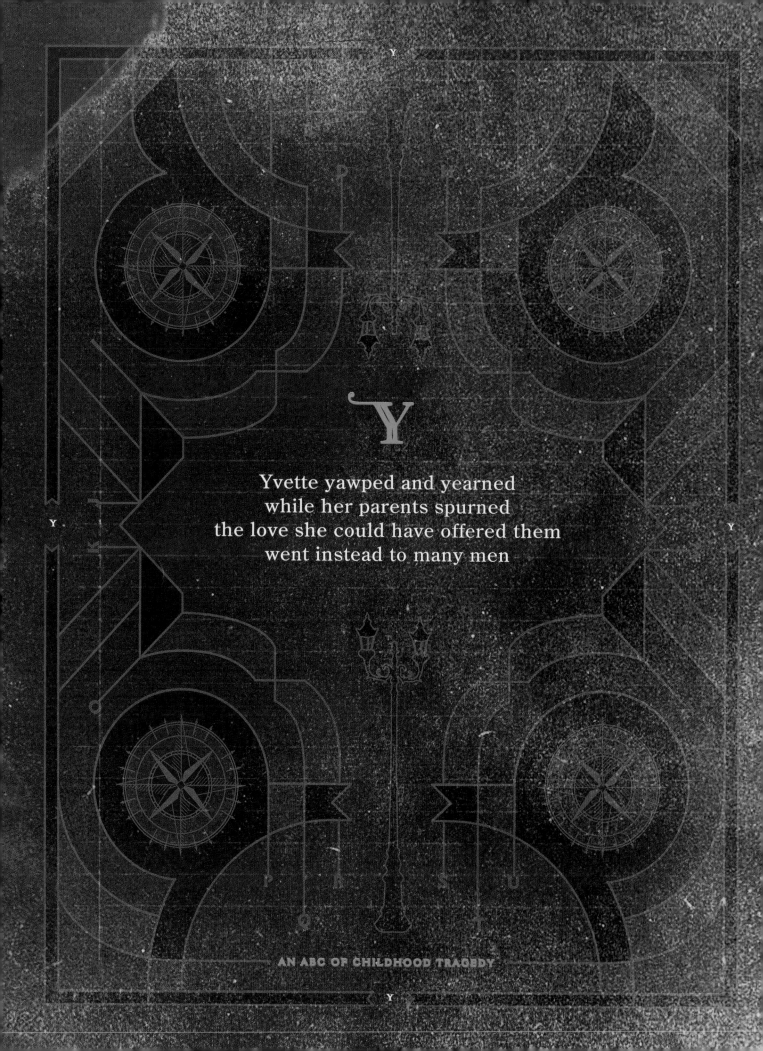

Y

Yvette yawped and yearned
while her parents spurned
the love she could have offered them
went instead to many men

YVETTE YAWPED AND YEARNED

Y

Z

Zachariah's vacuity
felt with acuity
came as a jolt
to his father
(the dolt)

ZACHARIAH'S VACUITY FELT WITH ACUITY

About
the *Author*

Dr. Jordan B. Peterson is the author
of the bestselling *12 Rules for Life:
An Antidote to Chaos, Beyond Order:
12 More Rules for Life,* and *Maps of
Meaning: The Architecture of Belief.*
He currently resides in Toronto, Canada,
with his wife, Tammy. More information
about Dr. Peterson is available
at jordanbpeterson.com.

About the *Illustrator*

Juliette Fogra, a fine art painter and graphic artist, was the illustrator of Dr. Peterson's *Beyond Order: 12 More Rules for Life*. She was born and raised in Riga, Latvia but currently resides in New York with her husband, Arthur, and their two children, Ariel and Noah. More information about Juliette is available at juliettefogra.me.